A MOP FOR POP

All inquiries should be addressed to:
Barron's Educational Series, Inc.
250 Wireless Boulevard
Hauppauge, NY 11788

International Standard Book Number 0-8120-4680-3

Library of Congress Catalog Card Number 91-13450

Library of Congress Cataloging-in-Publication Data

Erickson, Gina Clegg.
    A mop for pop / Gina Clegg Erickson and Kelli C. Foster :
illustrations by Kerri Gifford.
        p. cm.—(Get ready...get set...read!)
Summary: Illustrates graphically and in rhyme why lop-eared
rabbits don't belong in ice cream shops.
    ISBN: 0-8120-4680-3
    (1. Rabbits—Fiction   2. Stories in rhyme.)
I. Foster, Kelli C.   II. Gifford, Kerri, ill.   III. Title.   IV. Series: Erickson,
Gina Clegg. Get ready...get set...read!
PZ8.3.E787Mo   1991
(E)—dc20   91–13450
                                                     CIP
                                                     AC

PRINTED IN HONG KONG

20 19

GET READY...GET SET...READ!

A MOP FOR POP

by
Foster & Erickson

Illustrations by
Kerri Gifford Russell

BARRON'S

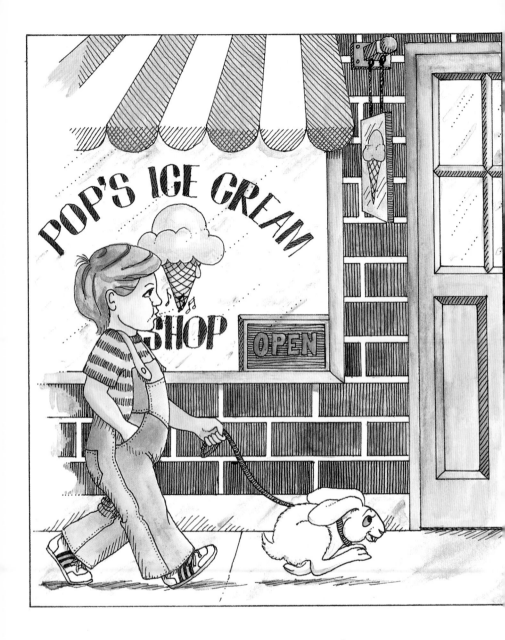

Here comes a lop.
It is a funny bunny.

A lop in the shop.

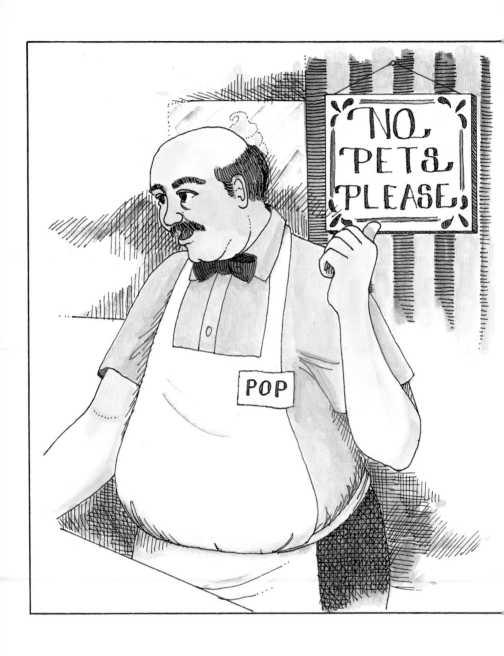

No lops in this shop!

No lops?

Hello, Pop!

Please, two on top. . .

Oh, no!
There goes the lop . .

and there goes Pop!

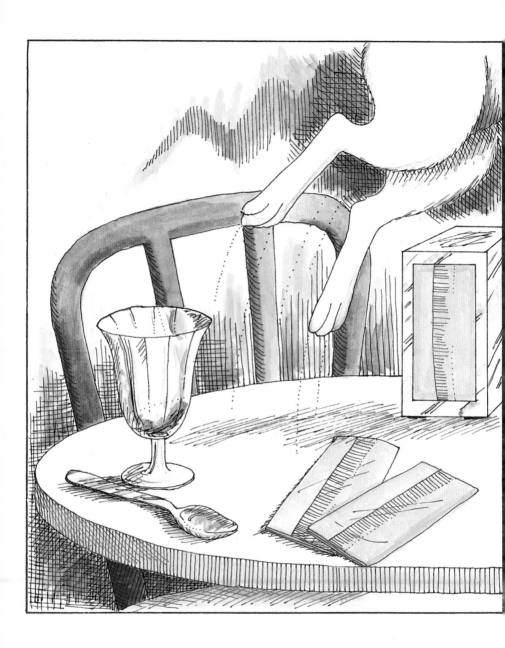

Stop, lop!
Do not hop.

Hop . . . hop . . . slop.

This must stop.
Where is that lop?

Plop, plop . . .
two drop on top of Pop.

Get a mop.
Where is the mop?

There is the mop!

What a funny lop-mop.

The End

The OP Word Family

lop
lops
Pop
top
hop
mop
plop
stop
drop
lop-mop
slop
shop

Sight Words

a
do
oh
of
the
two
here
what
comes
there
where

Dear Parents and Educators:

Welcome to *Get Ready...Get Set...Read!*

We've created these books to introduce children to the magic of reading.

Each story in the series is built around one or two word families. For example, *A Mop for Pop* uses the OP word family. Letters and letter blends are added to OP to form words such as TOP, LOP, and STOP. As you can see, once children are able to read OP, it is a simple task for them to read the entire word family. In addition to word families, we have used a limited number of "sight words." These are words found to occur with high frequency in the books your child will soon be reading. Being able to identify sight words greatly increases reading skill.

You might find the steps outlined on the facing page useful in guiding your work with your beginning reader.

We had great fun creating these books, and great pleasure sharing them with our children. We hope *Get Ready...Get Set...Read!* helps make this first step in reading fun for you and your new reader.

Kelli C. Foster, PhD
Educational Psychologist

Gina Clegg Erickson, MA
Reading Specialist

Guidelines for Using *Get Ready...Get Set...Read!*

Step 1.   Read the story to your child.

Step 2.   Have your child read the Word Family list aloud several times.

Step 3.   Invent new words for the list. Print each new combination for your child to read. Remember, nonsense words can be used (*dat, kat, gat*).

Step 4.   Read the story *with* your child. He or she reads all of the Word Family words; you read the rest.

Step 5.   Have your child read the Sight Word list aloud several times.

Step 6.   Read the story *with* your child again. This time he or she reads the words from both lists; you read the rest.

Step 7.   Your child reads the entire book to you!

Titles in the

Series:

SET 1

Find Nat
The Sled Surprise
Sometimes I Wish
A Mop for Pop
The Bug Club
BRING-IT-ALL-TOGETHER BOOKS
What a Day for Flying!
Bat's Surprise

SET 2

The Tan Can
The Best Pets Yet
Pip and Kip
Frog Knows Best
Bub and Chub
BRING-IT-ALL-TOGETHER BOOKS
Where Is the Treasure?
What a Trip!

SET 3

Jake and the Snake
Jeepers Creepers
Two Fine Swine
What Rose Does Not Know
Pink and Blue
BRING-IT-ALL-TOGETHER BOOKS
The Pancake Day
Hide and Seek

SET 4

Whiptail of Blackshale Trail
Colleen and the Bean
Dwight and the Trilobite
The Old Man at the Moat
By the Light of the Moon
BRING-IT-ALL-TOGETHER BOOKS
Night Light
The Crossing

SET 5

Tall and Small
Bounder's Sound
How to Catch a Butterfly
Ludlow Grows Up
Matthew's Brew
BRING-IT-ALL-TOGETHER BOOKS
Snow in July
Let's Play Ball